A S

Death at Jamestown

by Noe Venable

Don Johnston Incorporated
Volo, Illinois

2

Edited by:

Jerry Stemach, MS, CCC-SLP
Speech/Language Pathologist, Director of Content Development, Start-to-Finish® Books

Gail Portnuff Venable, MS, CCC-SLP
Speech/Language Pathologist, San Francisco, California

Dorothy Tyack, MA
Learning Disabilities Specialist, San Francisco, California

Consultant:

Ted S. Hasselbring, PhD
William T. Brian Professor of Special Education Technology, University of Kentucky

Graphics and Illustrations:

Photographs and illustrations are all created professionally
and modified to provide the best possible support for the
intended reader.

Narration:

Professional actors and actresses read the text to build
excitement and to model research-based elements of fluency:
intonation, stress, prosody, phrase groupings and rate.
The rate has been set to maximize comprehension for the reader.

Published by:

Don Johnston Incorporated
26799 West Commerce Drive
Volo, IL 60073

800.999.4660 USA Canada
800.889.5242 Technical Support
www.donjohnston.com

DON JOHNSTON

International Standard Book Number
ISBN 1-58702-764-X

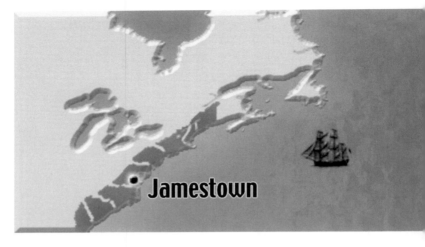

~Introduction~

May 24, 1610 Jamestown, Virginia

I write by the light of a single candle. I am cold and my body is heavy and numb. But my mind is full of pictures. Oh Virginia! For three years I have braved your shores. Now, my hand trembles as I remember everything that I have seen.

Let me introduce myself. My name is Jeremy Gower, and I was born in London, England. Three years have passed since I

left London in December 1606, and came to these strange shores. I know now that I will die here.

My dear family is far away in London. I have a father, a mother, and a sister. I will not see them again, unless God wills us to be together in heaven. But if you, dear reader, should ever meet them, give them these pages, so that they may hear what has happened to me, and to all of us Englishmen who came to this new world.

A Step into History

Chapter One

A Long Sea Voyage

This story begins long before my own miserable part in it. Some men in London started a company to explore the New World. This new world was called America, and she was said to be a land of wealth and possibilities.

Also, the company believed that just beyond the land called Virginia there was another ocean. If English explorers could discover the rivers that led to this ocean, they would be able to send ships to China without having to cross over any land. This would make it much easier to trade with China. Spain had already set up colonies in South America and Florida, and every time the Spanish ships returned to Spain, they were filled with gold and other treasures. The New World seemed ripe for the taking.

The Englishmen called their company the Virginia Company of London. They advertised in newspapers for men and boys to go to Virginia. "Virginia is a land of opportunity!" they said. "Go to Virginia and make your fortune."

"A land of opportunity!" I whispered to myself as I stood on the deck of the *Susan Constant.* The *Susan Constant* was the largest of the three ships that were going to carry us across the sea to the shores of the New World. There were also two smaller ships, the *Godspeed* and the *Discovery*. They followed close behind as we left the harbor just south of London and sailed down the River Thames and into the Atlantic Ocean.

I remember the fresh, salty air on my face. I remember my family waving from the dock. I thought I could see my mother holding a handkerchief to her face, so I guessed that she was crying.

"Is that your family?" said a voice.

I looked around and saw a boy standing next to me. He looked about 15, like me, but I could see that his life had been very different from mine. His clothes were so rumpled that I was sure they had never been washed or ironed. The boy was grinning.

I smiled back.

"My name's Anthony," he said. "And you?"

"Jeremy," I replied. "Jeremy Gower. Did your family come to see you off?"

"I haven't got one," said Anthony.

I was embarrassed, and I started to apologize.

"It's all right," he said. "I've gotten over it." He smiled again. "Exciting, isn't it!"

"Yes." Exciting didn't seem like a strong enough word. All my life I had read stories of great heroes, but I had never had a real adventure myself.

"Have you been around the ship?" asked Anthony. "Come on. Let's explore."

"Do you think we're allowed?" I asked.

"Allowed?" he cried. "We'll be trapped on board this ship for months! We might as well know our way around."

That was that. Anthony took my arm, and we were off. The *Susan Constant* had two masts. Its white sails flapped and billowed in the wind. I counted fifteen sailors who were busy up on the deck.

In the bow of the ship was a cabin for the sailors to sleep in. In the stern of the ship, there was another cabin. But when Anthony started to go into it, he ran right into a large man in a gray coat who was coming out.

"You're not allowed in here!" the man said in a huff. "It's Captain Newport's quarters. And watch where you're going." As he pushed his way past us, I recognized his face.

"That was Master Wingfield!" I said to Anthony.

"Who's that?"

"He's one of the men who founded the London Company," I said. "My father pointed him out to me once at a dinner party. Mr. Wingfield's not... well, my father says he's not very nice, but he's very important."

"Well then," said Anthony, "I'm glad I ran into him. Come on, let's have a look down below."

We climbed through one of the hatches in the deck and down a ladder to the tween deck. The tween deck smelled like manure, because under the tween deck was a place called the hold, where animals and livestock were kept, along with the ship's cargo of supplies and tools.

There were a number of rough-looking men down in the tween deck, playing cards and talking. Then we saw a boy who looked younger than we were, and we went over to him and asked his name.

"Sam Collier," said the other boy. "I'm page to Captain John Smith." Sam pointed to a man with a beard who was climbing up the ladder to the deck.

"I'll bet this is where we sleep," said Anthony.

"Where are the beds?" I asked.

Anthony laughed and pointed to some men who were napping on blankets spread out on the floor.

"All right then," I said. I was impressed. I'd never slept on a wood floor before, but I was excited to try it.

"You're a strange one, aren't you," said Anthony. "Say, why'd you decide to come on this ship?"

"Dunno, really," I said. "Father expects me to take over his shipping business. I guess it just seemed strange to me to run a shipping business without ever having been on a ship. Besides, I'd like to work. I mean *really* work. I'd like to use my hands."

"Would you?" said Anthony. He stared at me for a moment. Then, without saying a word, he turned around and started back up the ladder to the deck. I climbed after him, wondering what I had said to offend him.

Back on the deck, I followed him past a group of gentlemen and all the way to the railing of the ship. We turned up our collars to keep out the blustery wind. "I'm sorry," I said. "Did I say something to offend you?"

He turned around to look at me. "So you're looking for adventure," he said. "You're tired of your comfortable life so you've come here for a bit of adventure."

"Well, why did *you* come here?" I asked him.

"Why not?" he said.

And then he smiled. This time I noticed that a couple of his teeth were rotten, and I realized what those rotten teeth meant. I thought about the beggars I had seen on the streets of London. I thought about what Anthony's life must have been like in London, and I was ashamed.

Anthony figured that no distant shore, however dangerous it might be, could be worse than the life of a beggar on the streets of London.

Time would tell if he was right.

A Step into History

Chapter Two

Welcome to Virginia

The winds were not in our favor, so we spent the first five weeks of our journey within 20 miles of England's shore. As for me, I was sick of being at sea, and we hadn't even started out yet!

I can tell you that sleeping on a wood floor quickly lost its thrill. The tween deck smelled like sweat mixed with vomit and the smell of animals.

Soon, just going down there was enough to make me want to throw up.

There was a minister called Reverend Hunt on the ship who got so sick that Captain Newport offered to take him back home to London. Anthony and I were talking with a boy named Hugh up on the deck when Reverend Hunt walked by with Captain Newport and Master Wingfield.

"I'll not go home," said Reverend Hunt, coughing. "We are going to bring the Word of God to the poor savages in the New World. This voyage is God's will, and I, sir, shall do my part."

"I just hope it's not God's will for you to die on the way," grumbled Wingfield.

Anthony leaned over to me. "Someone ought to ask God to send a wind to blow us out of the harbor."

Poor Reverend Hunt was starting to turn green. We watched Captain Newport as he helped the Reverend over to the rail.

"Anthony," I said, "what have you heard about the savages?"

"I've heard that they eat people. They're cannibals with teeth three inches long," said Anthony.

"That's not what I've heard," said Hugh. "I've heard that they're as gentle and innocent as children. They don't know much, because they haven't any education, but they are happy to accept God into their lives when they have a patient teacher."

"*I* haven't got any education," said Anthony. "But I have a whole lot more sense than to expect the natives to come wading out to greet us."

It took us more than four months to get to Virginia. During that time, Wingfield and Captain Newport and some of the other gentlemen accused John Smith of mutiny. They made him stay down in the tween deck with a man to guard him. I asked Sam Collier what his master had done.

"They said he was plotting to murder us all and take over the ship," said Sam. "Of course he's innocent! It's the most ridiculous thing I've ever heard. The other men don't like him, that's all."

My goodness, I thought to myself. If we can't get along on a ship for a few months, what will it be like when we get to Virginia?

Oh Virginia! Enough talk of the voyage. Nothing can compare with the excitement I felt when our ships entered the Bay of Chesapeake, and I finally saw your shore for the first time.

The date was April 26, 1607.

"Land ho!" cried the sailors. It was early morning. We swarmed up the ladders of the tween deck to look.

"Can you believe it?" I asked Hugh.

"Well, lads, it's a beautiful sight, I grant you that," said Anthony.

"Yes," said a voice beside me. "A land of possibilities."

I turned around to see who had spoken. It was John Smith! This was the first time I had seen him up close. He was a short man with intense blue eyes and a strong, clear voice.

"Yes, they finally let me out, boys," said Smith with a laugh, "and you'll see that it's a good thing they did. Take care when we go ashore. Keep your wits about you."

Our three ships dropped their anchors out where the water was deep, and then Captain Newport's sailors rowed us to shore in small boats. I noticed that John Smith and a few other men were carrying muskets.

"It's all mud!" said Hugh, as we stepped onto the land. "It's a swamp!"

I grinned. After months at sea, this swamp looked more beautiful to me than all of the castles in England. Tall grasses waved in the fresh breeze. Sea birds flew in wide arcs over our heads.

"Look men, woods!" said a gentleman named George Percy. "Have you ever seen such fine trees?" Percy's lip trembled, and then I noticed that he was crying. "It's... it's... magnificent," he said.

Anthony started to laugh, and I elbowed him.

We spent that day exploring the shore and the nearby woods. I remembered Smith's words of warning as we picked our way through the trees and over the lush, creeping vines.

When it was just beginning to get dark, we headed back to the shore, where the sailors were waiting to row us back to the ships. Then we heard a shout.

"Savages!"

We spun around and looked back the way we had come. At first I didn't see anything. Then, slowly, I began to make out dark forms moving through the grasses. They were crawling on all fours, holding their bows in their mouths. A few of them had stood up and were already taking aim.

The men around me began to shout. I heard arrows whizzing through the air, but it was too dark to see clearly. I dropped to the ground and then I heard the sound of musket shots, so loud that my ears rang with pain.

I'm not sure how long it all lasted.

"Are they gone?" someone asked.

"I don't know," said another man.

Someone near me was screaming in pain. I looked around, trying to see in the darkness. A sailor was lying on the ground with an arrow sticking all the way through his leg. "Get it out!" he screamed. "Get it out of me!"

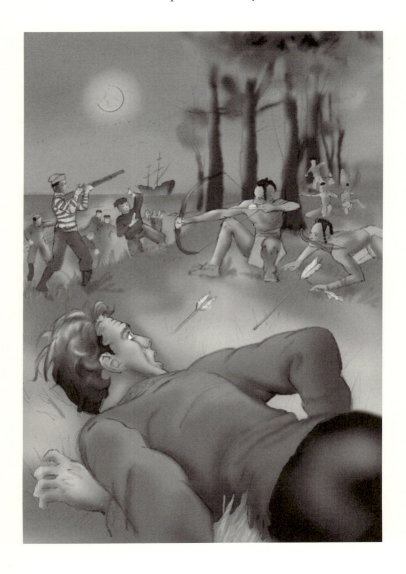

I saw someone yank the arrow out of the sailor's leg. A gentleman named Gabriel Archer was walking around holding his hands in the air. They were covered in blood.

Anthony was standing near me. "Welcome to Virginia," he said.

Chapter Three

The Council

Mr. Archer and the sailor both survived their wounds from the attack. Still, that night on the boat, it was hard for me to sleep. I kept thinking about those shadowy figures. How many men already lived in this wild new land? When I did manage to fall asleep, my dreams were dark and strange.

The next morning, Captain Newport took a party of men to explore the coast in a small boat. This time, the men wore metal armor and carried muskets. Newport wasn't taking any chances.

They returned that afternoon with news that they had discovered a large, flowing river that was wide enough and deep enough for the ships.

"We named it the James River," he said, "in honor of King James of England. We'll take the ships up the James. Along the way, we'll look for a good place to build a fort."

I now noticed that Newport was holding an envelope that looked official. It had been sealed with red wax. "As some of you may know," Newport continued, "our settlement here in Virginia will be led by a Council of men. The Company has already decided which men will be on the Council. We were instructed not to open this envelope until we arrived on the shore of Virginia. Now, with you all as witnesses, I shall break the seal and read the names."

There was a murmur of excitement among the gentlemen as Newport opened the envelope and began to read the list of names.

"Captain Newport," said Newport. "Bartholomew Gosnold, Captain of the *Godspeed*. John Ratcliffe, Captain of the *Discovery*. John Smith..."

There was a mumble of surprise from some of the gentlemen up front. "John Smith? The mutineer?" someone called out.

"He's not even a gentleman!" Percy whispered to Ratcliffe.

I looked over at John Smith. He looked smug.

"John Martin," Newport continued, "George Kendall and Master Wingfield. That's all. Reverend Hunt will serve as the advisor."

There was more muttering in the crowd. I could see that some of them who had not been chosen had expected to be on the Council.

"As some of you know," continued Newport, "I'll be leaving you in a couple of months to take the *Susan Constant* back to England for more supplies. At that time, you must look to the men of the Council to lead you."

We began to clap, and a few men cheered.

"Men of the Council," Newport went on, "our first duty will be to choose a president. All decisions will be made by a vote of the Council. Every man shall have one vote, except for the president, who shall have two votes."

The Council chose Master Wingfield to be president.

Then we set out up the James River in our three ships to look for a place to build our fort. The Company had sent instructions about that, too. The Company had said that we should "choose a place that was wholesome, and fertile, with rich soil and a healthy climate."

We had gone a few days up the river when the sailors noticed five natives running along the bank.

"Prepare the boat, men!" Newport called to the sailors as he put on his armor. "I'm going to speak with them."

Captain Newport called to the natives as the sailors rowed the boat to shore. The natives seemed frightened at first. Then Newport placed his hand on his heart. When the natives saw this, they set down their bows and arrows, and walked toward him. We watched them making signs in the air with their hands. Newport was making signs back. To my surprise, I thought I understood what they were saying to each other.

"Look. Newport is telling the natives not to be afraid — we are their friends," I said.

"Now the natives are inviting Newport to go somewhere with them," said Anthony.

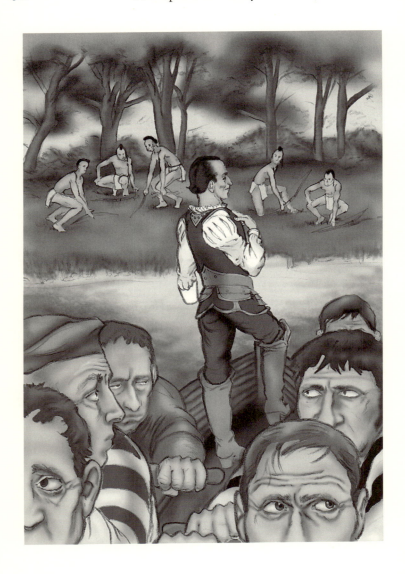

He was right. The natives had invited Newport to visit their village, which was called Kecoughtan. Newport sent the sailors to fetch George Percy and a few other gentlemen, along with John Smith and Sam, and they all followed the natives into the woods.

It was more than a week before Newport and his men returned. I was sure they had been killed. Several of us gathered around George Percy, who told us what they had learned from the natives.

"There are many different tribes here," Percy explained. "But there is one man who rules over all the tribes in this area. His name is Powhatan. The natives call him their Werowance."

"How were you treated?" asked a man.

"The Kecoughtans treated us very kindly," said Percy. "And they must have sent word to the other tribes along the river, because, as we traveled up the river, we were welcomed by many tribes.

We met many chiefs, but we have not yet met Powhatan," said Percy. "He lives in a village called Werowocomoco."

So this land was a nation! Just like England! It had kings and customs and towns. I had never met the King of

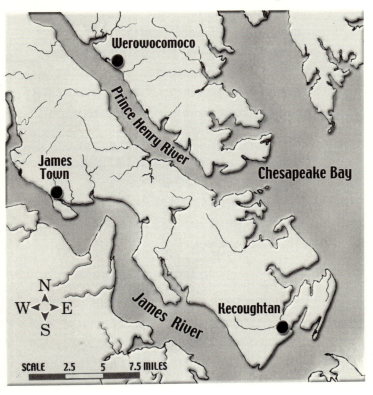

England. Would I ever lay eyes on the King of America?

That night was clear and bright with stars. A few of us lay out on the deck, looking up at the sky between the sails, long after most of the other men had gone to bed.

"Tell us about the savages," said Anthony.

"They danced for us," said Sam. "They made a circle and they stomped around it, howling like devils." He paused. "It's strange..." he said.

"What is?" I asked him.

"I had this feeling," said Sam, "that *they're* trying to figure *us* out, just like *we're* trying to figure *them* out. I wonder who's got who figured out the best?"

Chapter Four

A Wholesome and Fertile Place

Anthony, Hugh and I knew that it was the Council's job to choose the place to build the fort, but we kept a careful watch all the same, and we debated among ourselves, just as the Council was doing.

We passed a few places that Anthony and I agreed would be excellent spots to build a fort. We passed yellow fields and berry patches.

We explored woods where clear streams made their way between the trees, and long green vines coiled up the tree trunks. So I was surprised when I saw the place that the Council had chosen. It was a low, flat area of land about three miles long, that was called a peninsula because it jutted out into the river. Mosquitoes swarmed around us as we stepped onto the wet ground.

I would not have described it as wholesome or fertile.

"Well, how do you like that!" said Anthony. "They've set us down in another swamp."

That afternoon, the members of the Council were sworn in. That meant that each of them had to swear on the Bible that he would do his best to carry out the wishes of the London Company in the service of God and King James.

"I have decided to go against the London Company's wishes on one point," said Captain Newport. He turned and looked at John Smith. "You, sir, Mr. Smith, will not take a place on the Council."

John Smith stared straight ahead and did not say a word.

Then we all set to work. There was much to be done. Some men unloaded tools and supplies from the ships. Anthony helped other men get out the tents that we had brought. When they opened the tents, they had an unpleasant surprise. "They're full of holes!" cried Anthony. "They've been eaten by moths!"

"How did this happen?" Newport asked Wingfield.

"The Company bought tents that had been used on another expedition," said Wingfield, "but we were promised that they would be in good condition!"

These moth-eaten tents would be our only shelter until we could build something more permanent.

I chose to help the men who were chopping down trees to build a fence around our fort. I believe it was the hardest job of all.

Here, I must confess to you, dear reader, that this was the first time I had ever held an axe. I must also tell you that chopping down trees isn't as easy as it looks. The first time I swung the axe, the blade missed the tree entirely, and I ended up whacking the tree trunk with the handle instead. On my second try, I managed to hit the tree, but the blade didn't even cut through the bark. John Smith saw my struggle and came over. He didn't laugh, even though I must have looked rather foolish.

"Use your whole body," he said, "not just your arms. Swing from the waist, like this."

As we chopped down the trees, men came to take them over to Mr. Calthrop, who was in charge of building the walls of the fort. The men drove the logs into holes they had dug in the ground. It was slow, backbreaking work.

"It doesn't look like that fence would do much to protect us," said Anthony.

"It's not finished," I said, hopefully.

At one point, I heard John Smith talking to Captain Newport. "I wouldn't expect Wingfield to understand," said Smith, "but you have experience in these matters. The men need to practice defending the fort in case of another attack by the savages. They *must* be prepared."

"That's quite enough, Smith," Newport replied. "You're a fine explorer, but you're too quick to use force. The Company has instructed us to try to live at peace with the natives. If any natives see us preparing for battle, it may anger them and cause trouble."

After we had been working on the fort for about a week, Captain Newport decided that it was time to act on the next of the

Company's instructions. "It is the Company's wish that I spend the next two months exploring the James River. I will take a party of men with me. We will travel until we discover the river's end, which may very well be the ocean that lies on the other side of this land. At the same time, Captain Gosnold will take a party of men to look for gold in the hills."

So the two parties prepared to leave. Newport was taking 21 men with him. Most of them were sailors and gentlemen who were already experienced explorers. Gabriel Archer and George Percy were going. John Smith was going, too, and he was taking Sam.

Anthony and I walked over to help Newport's men load supplies into the boat.

"Good luck to you," I said to Sam.

Sam grinned. I could see that he felt important to be going on this adventure. "And good luck to you as well," he said.

"Thanks, we'll need it," said Anthony. "I don't know about you, Gower, but I don't even know how to fire a musket."

Chapter Five

The Natives Attack!

Master Wingfield and Stephen Calthrop stayed behind to supervise the work on the fort. During the day, we worked hard, and during the night, we did our best to sleep on the cold ground in our moth-eaten tents.

The fresh drinking water that we had brought on the boat was long gone, so now we had no choice but to drink the water from the river, which was full of slime and salt. The first time I tasted the water, I spit it out. "It's not drinkable!" I cried. But I learned to drink the water, just as I had learned to swing an axe.

In the week that followed, we had a number of friendly visits from the natives, who brought food to trade or to give as gifts, so I got to observe them firsthand.

The men were nearly naked. Each man wore a small square of leather around his waist. Some of the men had holes in their ears with animal bones in them.

The women wore nothing at all to cover their chests, and many of them had tattoos of fish or animals on their bodies.

Sometimes a group of young native girls came to the fort. They looked about nine or ten years old, and they walked around completely naked.

One of these girls seemed braver than the others. Her name was Pocahontas, and she was Powhatan's favorite daughter. One day, she came up to me while I was chopping down a tree. She stared at me with a big grin on her face. I was bad at chopping down trees when I was alone, and I was even worse when someone was staring at me. Especially when that person was a naked girl. I put down my axe and stared back at her.

Pocahontas walked right up to me and reached out to touch the shirt I was wearing. Then she covered her mouth. It looked like she was laughing at me. I looked down at my shirt, belt, breeches, long stockings and shoes. I must have looked strange to her, wearing all those clothes on such a hot day!

Pocahontas taught me one word from her language that day — "Wingapoh." It means friend. "Wingapoh," I called to her as she skipped away.

"Wingapoh!" she called back.

As the days passed, our progress on the fort was getting slower and slower. I began to feel tired all the time, and I could see that the same thing was happening to the others.

At first, Wingfield and Calthrop tried to take control of the situation. "What are you doing just standing there?" Wingfield would shout. "There's work to be done."

But whatever was happening to *us* was happening to *them* too. Soon, they seemed to want to lie down and rest, just like we all did. One afternoon, we were lying down in our tents, waiting for sleep to come to us, when we heard a battle cry!

"The natives are attacking!" someone shouted from outside the tent.

Terror struck us as arrows began to slice through the tents. I heard the thud of an arrow striking the chest of the man next to me. He screamed at the sight of his own blood spreading across his shirt.

We scrambled toward the door of the tent. A small boy, Nate Peacock, led the way. Then, horror! An arrow struck Nate's head, and he fell beneath our feet.

We stumbled outside just in time to see Wingfield's shocked face as an arrow flew right through his beard, just missing his face.

Wingfield and a few other men with muskets stood in front of the fort's unfinished fence. They fired shot after shot as more and more natives came rushing out of the woods toward us.

I heard a shout. It was Anthony. "Where are the muskets?" he cried. "Give us the muskets and show us how to fire them!"

"They haven't been unloaded from the ship yet," a man shouted back. "They're still in their crates!"

"Then we're lost!" cried Anthony.

I heard myself beginning to pray.

Suddenly, there was an explosion. Someone had fired a cannon from one of the ships! The cannonball whistled through the air and smashed into a tree, breaking a huge branch that fell right into the midst of the natives. This seemed to scare them. They began to shout, and then to scatter, and then, as quickly as they had come, they were gone.

I saw Hugh lying nearby, sobbing. I saw that there was an arrow stuck in his arm near his shoulder. I yanked it out with a jerk, and then I tore off my shirt and tied it around the wound to stop the bleeding.

The next day, when Newport and the others returned, they found seventeen men wounded and one boy dead.

"We killed some of the natives," said Calthrop, "But it's hard to know how many, because they dragged the bodies away with them."

That afternoon we had a funeral for Nate Peacock. When Reverend Hunt said the prayer for Nate's soul, his voice cracked with emotion. We lowered Nate's body into a small, shallow grave. Then the sailors fired the cannons again, in honor of Nate Peacock.

"John Smith," said Newport, "tomorrow you will begin training the men to fight. And I have changed my mind. You will be sworn in as a member of the Council."

Chapter Six

Enemies Within

Captain Newport and his men had returned from their expedition after only a week. They had not found the ocean. The river had ended in a waterfall, and they could go no further. Along the way, they had met many native tribes. The chiefs of these tribes had welcomed Newport's party with kindness.

When Wingfield heard this, he was furious. "They were only trying to keep you away from the fort so they could come here and slaughter the rest of us!" he cried.

Newport wasn't so sure. "There are many different tribes here," he said, "and these different tribes may each have different feelings about us."

Soon Gosnold and his men returned from their expedition as well. They had found gold! At least it looked like gold. It would have to be taken back to England for testing before anyone could be sure.

The return of these men lifted our spirits and we began work on the fort with new energy.

We built the fort out of pointed logs called pales. The pales were placed in three walls in the shape of a triangle. At the point where two walls came together, the logs made a half-circle called a bulwark. Each bulwark had a platform for a cannon and openings in the wall that were just wide enough for a musket to shoot through.

"From now on," said Newport, "the bulwarks must be guarded at all times."

We also began to build a few buildings inside the fort. We built a storehouse for our food supply and ammunition, and we started to work on a small church. It would be a long time before we would have homes to sleep in. Even the gentlemen of the Council had to sleep in the moth-eaten tents.

One day, I was on guard duty with Sam when we saw two natives approaching. "Wingapoh!" they cried.

Sam began to take aim with his musket. "Wait," I said. "Stop! 'Wingapoh' means friend! They come in peace!"

These two natives had a message for the men of the Council. By now, John Smith could understand enough of the native language to translate what they were saying. "The message is from Powhatan," said Smith. "Powhatan says he will try to keep the nearby tribes from attacking us."

The hope of peace with the natives filled us all with relief. The next day, Captain Newport and the sailors boarded the *Susan Constant* and the *Godspeed* to return to England for more supplies and to bring over more English settlers.

Now, dear reader, I must try to explain the events of those next months. When did it begin—the dreadful spiral downward into hunger and sickness that would take the lives of so many of our men? I think back to a conversation with Anthony, sometime in the hot, muggy month of August 1607.

"I think it's the water," said Anthony.

"The water?" I asked. We were sitting on the dusty ground, leaning on a tree.

"I think it's the water that's making us sick," said Anthony. "I think you were right. It's *not* drinkable."

I was too weak to answer him.

We had nearly run out of food. All that was left in the storehouse was some rotten barley that we had brought over from England. The grain had spent 26 weeks in the ship's hold, so now there were more worms than barley. Each day, four men had to share one small can of barley soaked in river water.

One by one, the men began to die. Some died of fever. They had caught a sickness called malaria that came from the mosquitoes. Other men died of starvation. Three or four men died each night. After a while, we stopped having funerals for them. When a man died, he was dragged out of the tents like a dead dog, and thrown in a hole on top of a heap of other bodies.

Throughout this time, Reverend Hunt continued to preach. The church that we were building was not much more than a shack, but Reverend Hunt never complained.

Those months were like a bad dream to me. At first I walked around in a daze. Then there came a time when I wasn't strong enough to walk, and I lay down and didn't know when I was awake and when I was asleep.

As more and more of the men of the colony died, the men of the Council began to fight among themselves most terribly.

Here is what I remember. Gosnold died. Then Smith, Martin, and Ratcliffe accused Wingfield and George Kendall of many small crimes, and locked them up on the *Discovery* to await trial. Then the Council elected Ratcliffe president. Shortly after that, Ratcliffe got angry with a man named John Read and decided to have him hanged.

But as Read stood on the gallows with a noose around his neck, he yelled, "Let me go! Someone on this Council is planning a mutiny! If you let me go, I will tell you what I know."

So they took Read down from the gallows, and he shouted, "It's George Kendall! He's planning to take the *Discovery* and return to England!"

From one of the bulwarks, Smith aimed a cannon at the *Discovery*. "Stay or sink in the river!" he shouted.

Kendall stayed. The other men of the Council accused him of treason and shot him dead. Wingfield was kept a prisoner on the *Discovery*.

I imagine that if it had gone on much longer, none of us would have lived through the summer. If starvation didn't kill us, we would surely have killed each other!

There were only forty of us who survived the summer. Among them were my friends, Anthony, Hugh, and Sam.

Then, as winter approached, birds began to fill the river. Anthony was the first one to notice. "Look!" he cried. "You'll never believe it! Swans!"

We ran to the river to look, and it was true. "Not only swans!" I cried. "Geese, ducks and cranes!"

"We're going to survive!" cried Hugh. "We'll eat well in these next weeks!"

How strange, I thought to myself. Once I would have looked at such birds and thought only of their beauty.

Chapter Seven

John Smith's Luck

In December, John Smith and a party of nine men left to explore the Chickahominy River on a large flat boat called a barge. But a few days later, three of the men returned to the fort alone.

"The others have been killed," cried one of the men, "and John Smith is surely dead as well!"

"Good Lord!" cried Ratcliffe. "What's happened?"

"We traveled up the river until we came to a place where trees had fallen and blocked our way," said the man. "The boat couldn't get past those trees, so Smith decided to continue up the river on foot. He took Robinson and Emry with him.

"While they were gone, four of the men grew weary of waiting in the boat, and they wanted to go ashore. A few moments after we dropped them off, we heard the cry of natives. We couldn't see what was happening, but we could hear everything. The natives wanted to know where John Smith had gone. They tortured our men until the men finally told them that Smith had gone upriver."

"Oh no," I heard Sam whisper beside me. "My master is dead!" I put my arm around the boy as he cried.

Three weeks went by. Then, one evening, Sam and I returned from gathering firewood and found John Smith sitting at the campfire, surrounded by the other men of the colony.

"We thought you were dead!" cried Sam.

"No, boys," said John Smith, laughing. "I'm not dead. My luck has been with me these past weeks."

We gathered round Smith to hear his story.

"As you know, I set out with Robinson and Emry to explore on foot. After a short way, we met two natives, and I hired them as our guides. I went on ahead with one of them, and I left Robinson and Emry with the other native to cook some meat for supper. We hadn't walked far when we heard the cries of more natives. They had found Robinson and Emry, and now they were coming after me.

"As 200 more natives came out of the trees to face me, I grabbed my guide and I held him in front of me like a shield," Smith continued. "The natives couldn't shoot me because they didn't want to kill one of their own people.

"This was my chance to escape," Smith explained. "I began to back up very slowly. My luck wasn't with me at this point, however. I backed us right into the Chickahominy swamp, and our feet got stuck in the ooze!

"Just then, another native stepped into the clearing," Smith went on. "I could see at once that he was the leader."

"Powhatan?" I asked.

"Opechancanough," he replied. His voice was deep and strong.

"'You're Powhatan's brother?' I asked. 'King of the Pamunkeys?'

"Opechancanough nodded his head. Then he called two of his men over, and they pulled us out of the swamp and took me prisoner.

"For the next few days, Opechancanough and his men marched me along the James River, showing me off to the other tribes who live there, until we reached a village called Werowocomoco. This village is the home of Powhatan's tribe," explained Smith. "About 200 native men, women and children came out of their huts to watch as I was led into Powhatan's hut, which was called a longhouse.

"There was Powhatan sitting before a fire," continued Smith. "Around his shoulders he wore a great robe of raccoon skins, with all the tails hanging down. Beautiful young native women in white feather headdresses were sitting on either side of him and in a line behind him. I've never seen a man look more powerful.

"As I stood before him, one of the women brought me a bowl of water to wash

my hands, and another woman brought
me feathers to dry them.

"Then, two men took me by my arms
and led me over to two large stones that
had been placed in front of Powhatan, and
they motioned for me to lie down with my
head on the stones," said Smith. "The
men picked up huge clubs, and I thought
they were going to beat my brains out."

"So what happened?" asked Sam
anxiously.

"Well, a young girl stood up in the
corner of the room and walked over to me.
Later, I learned that she is Powhatan's
favorite daughter, and her name is
Pocahontas. No one said a word as
Pocahontas leaned down and touched her
face to mine. Then the men put down
their clubs and everyone in the room let
out a great shout.

"Now I was allowed to stand up.
Pocahontas stood beside me and we faced
Powhatan.

"Powhatan pointed to Pocahontas and said a word that means 'daughter,' " said Smith. "Then he pointed at me, and said a word that means 'son.' "

Suddenly Ratcliffe interrupted Smith. "What was the meaning of all this?" he asked.

"I don't know," said Smith. "But from then on, Powhatan started calling me his son. He said that he wanted to meet the great chief of the English. He asked me the name of our chief.

" 'Our leader is named Newport.' I replied. 'He is across the water in England, but when he returns, I will ask him to meet with you.'

"Powhatan seemed pleased with this, and then he asked me to do my first duty as his son."

"What was that?" asked Sam.

"He asked me to give him guns," said Smith. "So I told him that we would give him two of our strongest guns. We would give him two cannons. Two of Powhatan's men came back to the fort with me to get them."

"You're a fool!" cried Ratcliffe.

Smith laughed. "No," he said. "There's nothing to worry about. I knew that the natives would never be able to lift those cannons. They had to return to the village empty-handed."

Ratcliffe didn't laugh. "Well," he said, "that's a fine story you've told us, Mr. Smith. Now I have some news for you. As you know, John Martin has been sick for some time, and is quite unable to vote. As president, I have appointed Master Gabriel Archer to the Council." Archer stepped up to join Ratcliffe.

"That's right," said Archer. "And we, the men of the Council, do hereby accuse you of the murders of Robinson, Emry, and the other men who died while you were their leader! Tomorrow you will be hanged."

Chapter Eight

Fire!

John Smith was not hanged. His luck came through for him again. Smith was standing on the gallows with the noose around his neck, when an English ship appeared, making its way up the river.

"God be praised!" cried Reverend Hunt.

Captain Newport had returned from England in a new ship called the *John and Francis.*

"Good Lord!" cried Newport, when he saw Smith standing on the gallows. "Get him down at once! Where is Wingfield? Where are the men of the Council? What in the name of heaven has happened in these months I've been gone?"

Newport did his best to sort out the confusing mess that the Council had become. He pardoned John Smith, but he kept Wingfield locked up on the *Discovery*, where he had been for several months.

When Captain Newport spoke to us, I could hear the concern in his voice. More than half of us had died during these first months in this "land of opportunity." Those of us who had survived were sickly and skinny.

"Have courage, men," said Newport. "I have brought a great deal of food and new supplies, and sixty able-bodied men and boys to help us build our city of Jamestown."

We all cheered at this good news.

"But I have some bad news as well," Newport continued. "There was another ship with us, the *Phoenix*, and she sailed into a fog and was lost."

"We will remember the lost men of the *Phoenix* in our prayers," said Reverend Hunt.

"There's another thing," said Newport. "The mineral samples that I took back to England were examined. They are not gold. But never fear. There must be gold in these hills somewhere, and we will keep searching until we find it."

That afternoon, we began to unload the supplies from the ship to bring them into the storehouse. I swear to you that food had never looked so good to me in my life. There was smoked meat, bread, sacks of flour and wheat and oats and so much more!

"Can you believe it?" cried Anthony. He was holding a small sack of flour and dancing with it like it was a girl.

"Careful," I laughed, "or your dancing partner will spring a leak!"

In those next days, the fort came to life with activity. Newport had brought some real carpenters with him, and they set about strengthening the walls of the storehouse. They also began work on a sturdy new church with a fine cross on its roof. Reverend Hunt beamed as he watched them working.

"At last, I'll have a place to put my library!" he said to Smith. "I can manage through the rain and weather, but my books! My books need a good, dry home!"

With a storehouse full of food, a good start on a new church, and new men to help us, our spirits were high. One day, Anthony, Hugh and I went out to gather firewood with a new, younger boy named Henry.

"Look," I said to Henry, "try to choose branches that are dry and brown. The branches that are still green in the middle won't burn so well."

Henry looked at me strangely.

Anthony broke into a laugh. "You idiot!" he said to me, "everyone knows how to gather firewood."

"Oh," I said. "I'm sorry, Henry. You see, *I* didn't know when I came." I suddenly saw how much I had changed in these few months, and I began to laugh at myself. It was a good hearty laugh that made me feel better than I had felt in a long time.

I stopped walking for a moment, and the other boys stopped with me. We stood, taking deep breaths of the chilly, crisp air. A bird was singing in a tree.

"It's funny, isn't it," said Hugh.

"What?" I asked.

"I was thinking about God," he said. "Those weeks were so terrible, when everyone was dying around us. And then, Newport arrived just in time to save John Smith from being hanged, just as if it was..."

"A miracle?" said Anthony.

"If it wasn't a miracle," I said, "then it was the best luck *I've* ever seen. I wonder if John Smith realizes..."

But I didn't get to finish my sentence. I was interrupted by the sound of an explosion! It had come from the direction of the fort. We all looked at each other. Then we heard loud popping sounds, as loud as twenty muskets going off at once. And then we heard a shout.

"Fire!"

We dropped the branches we had collected and ran.

When we got to the fort, we could hardly believe our eyes. The fort was completely ablaze! Black smoke was rising in terrifying clouds from the roofs of the buildings. Flames were licking at the walls of the fort.

"The storehouse!" cried Anthony. "Look!"

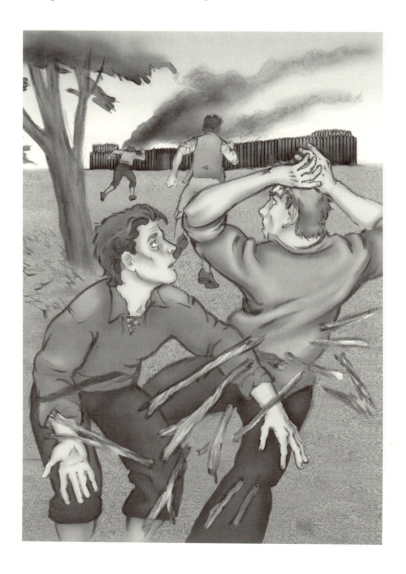

Now I knew where the explosion had come from. The fire was blowing up the gunpowder in the storehouse!

"Our food!" I cried.

"Boys!" yelled Smith, "grab a bucket and join the line."

The men had made a bucket line to the river. The man who was nearest to the river filled buckets with water and passed them down the line to the men who were nearest to the fort, and they would slosh the water onto the burning buildings.

But despite our best efforts, the fire only seemed to get more furious. It raged on into the night.

I will never forget the sight of Reverend Hunt, as he stood in the bucket line, watching the flames dancing on the roof of his fine new church. Just that day, he had put his precious books inside.

Now they were burning. His face was shining with sweat in the heat of the fire, and his eyes were full of tears.

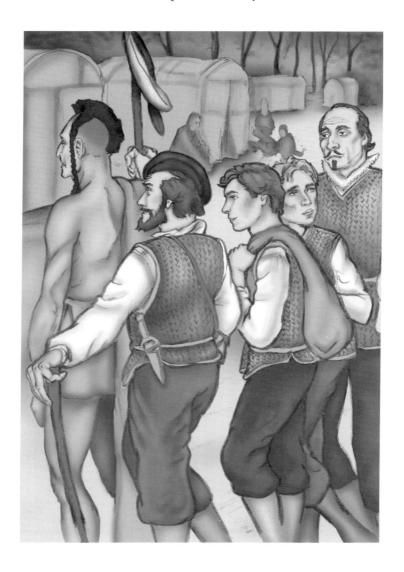

Chapter Nine

Trading

The fire destroyed everything we had in the fort. We lost all our food and ammunition. We even lost our blankets and extra clothes. The only things that survived were the few things that had not yet been unloaded from the ship.

Pocahontas came many times that winter, bringing us baskets of corn, meat, and bread. But it wasn't enough.

"We must go to Powhatan," John Smith said to Newport. "Powhatan has been wanting to meet you.

We must go to him and we must get him to trade," said Smith.

There were about thirty men who volunteered for the expedition. My friends and I were among these men.

We started down the James River and then traveled up the Prince Henry River. Newport didn't want to take any chances. For protection, we wore light quilted armored vests, called "jacks," that had been stored on board the *John and Francis.* When we arrived in Werowocomoco, Newport said, "I'll stay on board the ship with my sailors. Smith, you take a party of men and go ahead to make sure that we will have no trouble."

I joined Smith's party. Native men from Werowocomoco came to meet us at the shore, and they led us through the village to Powhatan's longhouse.

Smith told five of his men to remain outside and stand guard, while the rest of us walked into the longhouse.

Powhatan looked every bit as powerful as Smith had said. The chief sat on a mat, with one woman standing on his right, and another woman on his left. As we entered, he did not stand, but stretched out his hand toward us.

Two men stepped forward and rolled out a mat at the feet of John Smith. Smith sat down in front of Powhatan. Then Powhatan began to speak to Smith in the native language.

Powhatan seemed upset that Captain Newport hadn't come to see him. Smith seemed to be offering some kind of explanation.

Finally, Smith turned to us. "Powhatan has invited us to feast with his people. Tomorrow morning, he will meet with Captain Newport."

What a feast we had that night! We sat around a fire as the women laid huge platters of food on the ground in front of us. Everyone shared these platters and we ate with our hands.

After dinner, the natives made a circle around the fire. Then they began to dance, stomping their feet on the ground, and shaking rattles. As they danced, they chanted and shouted. At first, the chanting sounded strange to me, but then I began to hear the music in it.

"It's quite beautiful," Anthony said quietly.

The fire was warm and pleasant, and the dance continued long into the night.

The next morning, Newport came ashore to meet Powhatan to begin trade with him. Smith translated as the two men spoke. The first things they traded were people! Newport gave Powhatan a young boy named Tom Savage. "This boy is my son," said Newport, "and he will stay here with you to learn more of your ways and customs." We all knew that Tom Savage wasn't really Newport's son. He was just a poor young boy with no education.

"Powhatan would like to give you his son, Namontack, in return," said Smith. A young man stepped forward.

"I thank you, Powhatan," said Newport. "We will bring Namontack back to England with us. I'm certain that the people of our land will be eager to meet a real prince of Virginia."

Then Newport began to trade the items that he had brought to the village.

"Powhatan says he knows that you, Newport, are the great chief of the English," said Smith, "just as Powhatan is the great chief of the natives. So he asks you not to trade these little trinkets one by one, the way you trade with his people. He asks you to put down all of your goods, and he will give you what he thinks they are worth. This is how great chiefs should trade." Smith paused for a moment and then, in the same tone of voice, he said, "Be careful, Newport. He's trying to cheat you."

"Smith, you are here only as my interpreter," said Newport. "I will make the decisions here." Newport looked at the chief. "Yes, Powhatan! We will trade like great kings. Men, lay out our objects to trade."

The men laid out everything that Newport had brought. Powhatan studied the pile and then had his men bring out five bushels of corn.

"We could eat that much corn in one day!" said my friend Hugh.

Newport looked as if he wasn't sure what to do next.

Suddenly, Smith stepped forward. He reached into his pocket and pulled out a handful of blue beads. He spoke in both the native language and in English. I could see that he wanted Newport to hear what he was saying.

"I have one more thing to trade," said Smith. "These blue beads are the color of the sky and they are very rare. They have magic in them."

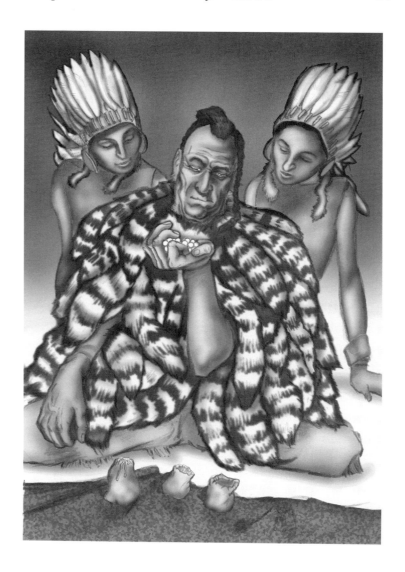

Powhatan took a few of the beads in his hands. His women leaned in closer to look.

Powhatan offered Smith another bushel of corn.

"You insult me!" said Smith. "These beads are worn only by the greatest chiefs and kings in the world. For all these beads, I would not take less than 300 bushels of corn. I will take back the beads."

Powhatan didn't seem to want to give the beads back to Smith. He rolled them around in his hand, as if he had never seen anything like them before. Then he motioned to his men to bring in 300 more bushels.

So we left Werowocomoco with 305 bushels of corn.

As we made our way back to Jamestown, Newport sometimes spoke to the other gentlemen who had come along, but to John Smith, he did not say a single word.

Newport had been planning to return to England soon to pick up more colonists and more supplies. But instead, he took a party of men to hunt for gold in the mountains. While they were gone, Newport's sailors stayed at the fort, eating our food and trading with the natives.

When Newport finally left for England, he took with him buckets full of shiny metal that looked like gold. He also took Wingfield and Archer with him.

Then, a few months later, on April 20, a ship appeared on the river. "Arm yourselves!" cried Sam, who was standing guard. "It may be the Spanish."

But it wasn't a Spanish ship. It was the *Phoenix* — the ship that had been lost in the fog on Christmas Eve! The men on board the *Phoenix* had had many adventures since that night. They had returned to the West Indies to stock up on supplies. The *Phoenix* brought forty new settlers and a boatload of supplies.

Chapter Ten

All
Hail Powhatan,
King of England

That fall, the men of the Council elected John Smith president of Jamestown.

Not long after that, Captain Newport returned from England on a ship called the *Mary and Margaret*. He brought with him more supplies, and seventy new settlers. Two of these settlers were women!

One of them was the wife of one of the gentlemen. The other woman was her maid, Anne Buras. I leave it to you to imagine how excited our men were to have a woman among them. I heard that seventeen men asked Miss Buras to marry them during her first week in Jamestown!

Newport also brought back Powhatan's son, Namontack, and some gifts for Powhatan.

"I have news to give you," said Newport. "First of all, the metal that we took back was not gold. The other news is that the London Company has decided to make Powhatan a King of England. Maybe this will encourage the natives to help us."

A few of the men cheered.

"Unload the gifts, men!" Newport called to the sailors.

I watched in amazement as an enormous bed was raised up onto the deck of the ship, and then loaded onto a barge

to be carried to shore. The bed was so big
that we thought the barge might sink.
Newport had also brought a cheap copper
crown, a red suit, and a fancy pair of
shoes which he showed to John Smith.

"Are you a fool?!" cried Smith.
"Don't you see? The more gifts we give to
Powhatan, the more gifts he will expect!"

"I've heard enough out of you!"
snapped Newport. "I have orders from the
London Company. Tomorrow you will go
to Werowocomoco, and you will tell
Powhatan that he must come to the fort at
Jamestown for his crowning."

Smith had no choice. He went to
Werowocomoco. When he returned, he
brought a message but no Powhatan.

"Powhatan thinks that perhaps you do
not understand," said Smith. "Powhatan
says that he is *already* a king, and this is
his land. He's about to go on a trip to
visit some of his tribes. He says that he
will wait eight days to receive your gifts.
He will not come to the fort."

So we would have to bring the crown to Powhatan, and we would have to hurry. We loaded the enormous bed back onto the barge. Newport traveled by land with a party of fifty men to guard him. Anthony and I were among these men. We carried muskets, and, by now, we were quite good at firing them.

The crowning of Powhatan seems like a crazy dream to me when I think of it now.

Powhatan looked just as powerful as I remembered him. But instead of sitting on mats, Powhatan sat on his new bed.

"It can't be a real crowning without an archbishop," George Percy said.

"I'll be the archbishop," replied Newport.

When Smith told this to Powhatan, the chief asked a question, which Smith translated.

"Powhatan wants to know what an archbishop is," said Smith.

"Tell him that the archbishop is someone from the church who crowns the King," said Newport. "Tell him that he must now take off his shoes and his deerskin cape, and then he must put on these new red clothes and shoes."

But when John Smith explained this to Powhatan, Powhatan only shook his head.

"He thinks that these clothes look foolish," said Smith, "and he cannot believe that this is really what English kings wear."

It was Namontack who convinced Powhatan to put on the clothes by telling him that yes, this really *was* what English kings looked like.

Now Powhatan was standing up.

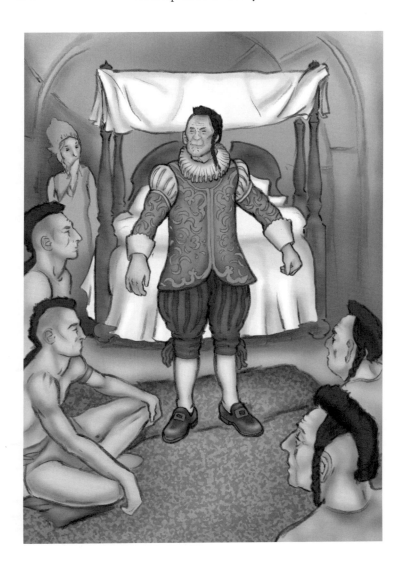

"I will now crown you King of England," said Newport. "Bow your head to receive the crown."

Newport held out the cheap copper crown, but Powhatan refused to bow his head. No amount of arguing could convince him. Finally, Smith and two other Englishmen, who were standing nearby, pushed down hard on Powhatan's shoulders, and Newport managed to get the crown on his head.

"All hail Powhatan, King of England," cried Newport.

"Huzzah! Huzzah!" we all shouted.

The natives seemed startled and confused by all of our shouting. But they were even more startled when the sounds of fifty musket shots exploded right outside the longhouse. They screamed and tried to run outside as Newport tried his best to explain that guns were often fired in England to honor a new king. When everybody finally calmed down, Newport brought up the next item of business.

"Now that you are a King of England, Powhatan, you must join us in serving his Majesty, King James," said Newport, smiling. "As your first duty, we ask you to give us guides who will help us explore the land just beyond your village."

Powhatan did not smile. He sat down once again upon his new bed, and then he spoke to Smith.

"Powhatan says no," said Smith. "He says that your only guide will be Namontack. He also offers you gifts. You may have his old shoes and his cape, and eight bushels of corn."

That was that. We headed back to Jamestown, bringing with us Powhatan's old shoes and cape, and the eight bushels of corn. A few of the gentlemen who had just come from England seemed pleased with our accomplishment. "Good for you, getting that crown on his head!" said one gentleman to Newport.

We had done what the company had asked us to do, and that was about the only good thing that I could think of to say about it.

Chapter Eleven

To Conquer Is to Live

That winter, Captain Newport returned to England to bring back another load of settlers.

Meanwhile, at Jamestown, new colonists meant many more mouths to feed. John Smith did all he could to find the food that we needed to survive.

His method was simple, but it took a madman to do it.   Smith would take a party of men to visit a tribe. If the tribe didn't want to trade with them, Smith and his men would threaten the natives with guns and swords and take everything they had.

Then one day, a native man came to the fort with a message from Powhatan. I heard Smith talking to Matthew Scrivener about the message. Scrivener was a man who had recently been added to the Council.

"Powhatan wants a house to put his bed in," said Smith.

"He says that if we send men to build him a house, he will fill our entire ship with corn."

"An entire ship full of corn!" cried Scrivener. "That's more food than we've had in weeks!"

"Yes, but I don't trust Powhatan," said Smith. "I don't believe he has a whole shipload of corn, since there's been almost no rain at all and their harvest has been poor. But if he does have that much corn sitting around, I'm sure we can find another way to get our hands on it. I have a plan. We'll send the men to start building the house. Powhatan will think that he has won, so he'll let his guard down. Then, we will strike and steal the corn!"

So Smith sent four carpenters to Werowocomoco. Then he set off with another party of men to steal Powhatan's harvest of corn.

One afternoon a couple of weeks later, two of the carpenters, Adam and Francis, came back to Jamestown. They went to the man who was guarding the storehouse. "Smith sent us," they said. "He needs some tools and fresh clothing."

The guard at the storehouse gave Adam and Francis the things they had asked for. It was late in the afternoon, so Adam and Francis decided to spend the night at the fort, and return to Werowocomoco in the morning.

That night, I woke up to the sound of a harsh whisper in my ear. "Gower! Wake up!"

It was Anthony! I was half asleep, but I followed him out of the hut and into the cold night air.

There, Anthony looked around to make sure nobody could hear him.

"I'm leaving," he said.

"What?"

"Shhh!" he said. "We haven't much time. I came to say goodbye."

"But where are you going?" I asked.

"To Powhatan," said Anthony. "He has promised a good life to all Englishmen who will leave Jamestown and join the natives. Adam and Francis didn't really come from Smith. Powhatan sent them to get tools and weapons to bring back to Werowocomoco."

"That's stealing!" I said.

Anthony stared at me for a moment. "Stealing?" he said. "Stealing? Don't be an idiot, Gower! Everyone's stealing! Don't you see? We steal from the natives. The natives steal from us. Stealing is what we do to each other."

I was quiet for a little while. "I can't go with you," I said.

"I know," said Anthony. "I know you well enough to know that you won't come with me. But I also know that I can trust you not to tell anyone about our conversation tonight."

I could only nod in agreement.

"Good-bye," he said. "Luck be with you, Jeremy Gower."

So Anthony and a few other men from the colony went with Adam and Francis to join Powhatan's tribe. They had stolen 300 hatchets, fifty swords, and eight muskets.

I think I began to cry as I watched them sneak out of the fort. I knew that it was wrong to go and join the natives. It *was* wrong, wasn't it? The more I tried to think about it, the more confused I became.

Smith returned about a week later. The Council had sent a man to find him and tell him what had happened. Smith was furious. But he had more bad news of his own. We all gathered around him.

"I have brought us corn," he said. "But it is much less than I expected. And I didn't get it from Powhatan. When I got to Werowocomoco, the place was deserted. Powhatan had left the village with all of his people."

So now the people of Werowocomoco were gone, and Anthony was gone with them. I would never see him again.

In the weeks that followed, a dark cloud hung over me. Our food supply was full of worms. The natives had hidden all their food in the woods so that Smith and his men couldn't steal it.

We had to live off what we could find on our own. We hunted squirrels and turkeys, and any other beasts that we could catch.

In August of that year, more ships came from England. The ships docked at Jamestown, and we watched as more than 400 new settlers spilled out onto the shore. Ratcliffe, Martin, and Archer were among these men. Captain Newport was nowhere to be seen.

"Newport was on board the seventh ship, the *Sea Venture*," said Ratcliffe. "We sailed into a hurricane on our way here, and the *Sea Venture* was lost."

We were glad the ships had brought new supplies from England, but where were all these people going to live? By now we had built some huts to sleep in, but there were already six or more men sharing each hut. Smith had a plan, as always. But this would be the last plan that he would make for the people of Jamestown.

Smith went up the river on a ship to try to buy a village from Parahunt, who was one of Powhatan's sons. But on his way back from buying the village, one of Smith's bags of gunpowder exploded and burned him badly, all over his stomach and his thighs.

Smith survived. But he was too badly injured to stay at Jamestown. He had to return to England.

The last time I saw John Smith, Sam and some other men were carrying him onto the ship that would take him back to England. As they passed, I was surprised to see Smith turn his head and speak to the group that had gathered to see him off. His words were clear.

"To conquer is to live, men," he said. "That is my motto, and it must be yours. Take this land! Make it a place where any man can become a great man. To conquer is to live!"

Chapter Twelve

The Starving Time

I have now nearly reached the end of my sad tale. Oh, such horrors I must now tell you about!

When John Smith left in October, our food supplies were almost gone. George Percy was elected president of Jamestown. There were now 500 English men and women in Virginia.

Then came the winter, and with it
came a terrifying truth: we were going to
starve.

Hunger bites at me like a starving
dog. All around me, people are dying.
They die slowly and painfully. They
shrink away until they turn into walking
skeletons. When they die, we drag them
out one by one and lay them on the
ground. We no longer have the strength
to dig a grave.

When the night is quiet, the sound of
moaning drifts through our desperate
town like a wind. But last week, I heard
a cry that rose far above all the others.

"God is dead!"

I crawled to the door of my hut to see
a bony figure staggering by. The figure
looked like it was made out of sticks. It
shook its fist and moaned, and as it
passed, I looked into its hollow eyes.

"Hugh!" I cried. It was my friend,
Hugh!

Hugh looked at me, but didn't seem to see me. He just turned and went on screaming. "God is dead! No living god would allow people to suffer as we are suffering."

I heard that he ran into the woods, where he was killed by natives. Another man died that same night. Some men from the village found his body not twenty feet from Hugh's. The natives had killed him, too.

Oh! I do not know how to explain what I am going to write next, so I must just write it, and leave it to you, dear reader, to decide what it means.

The dogs tore apart poor Hugh's body. They tore him to shreds, and ate every last bit of flesh from his bones. But for some reason the dogs didn't touch the other man, even though his body had more flesh on it than Hugh's did.

The rest of this story is for you, God, if you are there. May you hear this and have mercy on us! On all of us!

In these last weeks, people have begun to eat the bodies of the men who have died. They have eaten the bodies of natives, and they have eaten the bodies of Englishmen. One man ate his wife. For that, George Percy said that the man would die by torture. But I cannot imagine a torture worse than living in this cruel place.

Yesterday, two English ships arrived, led by Captain Newport. We thought for a moment that they had come with supplies, and we ran from the fort, crying out, "We are starved!"

But oh horror! Newport's ship, the *Sea Venture*, had been wrecked on the island of Bermuda. Newport and his men had used the pieces of the *Sea Venture* to build these two new ships. They brought 148 new settlers, and no food.

I know now that this will be the end. I lie here in my hut by the light of the cold moon. Questions burn in my mind. What is this new world? Who will it belong to?

I cannot know.

Good night, dear reader. With this, I leave you.

—Jeremy Gower

May 24, 1610

~ Bibliography ~
Death at Jamestown

Selected Resources

Bridenbaugh, Carl. *Jamestown 1544-1699*. New York: Oxford University Press, 1980.

Fritz, Jean. *The Double Life of Pocahontas*. Toronto, Canada: General Publishing Co. Limited, 1983.

Gleach, Frederic W. *Powhatan's World and Colonial Virginia—A Conflict of Cultures*. Nebraska: University of Nebraska Press, 1997.

Hume, Ivor Noel. *The Virginia Adventure: Roanoke to James Towne, An Archaeological and Historical Odyssey*. Virginia: University Press of Virginia, 1994.

Karwoski, Gail Langer. *Surviving Jamestown*. Atlanta, Georgia: Peachtree Publishers, Ltd, 2001.

Kupperman, Karen Ordahl. *Indians and English: Facing off in Early America*. Ithaca and London: Cornell University Press, 2000.

Lemay, J. A. Leo. *The American Dream of Captain John Smith*. Virginia: University Press of Virginia, 1991.

Mossiker, Frances. *Pocahontas*. New York: Alfred A. Knopf, 1976.

Percy, George. "A Trewe Relacyon, Virginia from 1609 to 1612," *Tyler's Quarterly Historical and Genealogical Magazine 3 (1922)*: 259-82, 1922.

Smith, John. *Captain John Smith's History of Virginia, Edited By David Freeman Hawke*. Indianapolis, New York: The Bobbs-Merrill Company Inc., 1970.

Woodward, Grace Steele. *Pocahontas*. Oklahoma: University of Oklahoma Press, 1969.

Web Sites

"Jamestown Rediscovery." Jamestown, VA: Association for the Preservation of Virginia Antiquities, 1997-2001. http://www.apva.org/jr.html

~ Author ~

Noe Venable

Noe Venable has been writing and performing since childhood. As a teenager, she wrote a play for young people which won a national award and which was performed by several different theater companies. Noe went to college to study playwriting, but she became interested in studying about history and music as well. She has recorded three CD's of her own music, and written several plays and several hundred songs.

Noe has also taught classes in literature, drama, and puppet making in summer school programs. She directed the production of *A Midsummer Night's Dream*, a play by William Shakespeare.

Noe lives in the San Francisco Bay Area. She often travels around the United States with her band performing her music.

~ Narrator ~

Joe Sikora

Joe Sikora was born in Chicago, Illinois. He has performed on stage in many theatres in Chicago, including the Goodman Theatre, the Chicago Shakespeare Theatre, the Lookingglass Theatre and the Shattered Globe. Joe has also been a boxer.

Joe now lives in Los Angeles, California where he works as a film and television actor. He has appeared in many films, including *Rudy, My Best Friend's Wedding, The Watcher* and *Ghost World.* He has appeared on television in *Turks, Early Edition, Walker, Texas Ranger, Missing Persons* and *Movie Stars.*

Joe Sikora is also the narrator of *Against All the Odds* and *Death at Jamestown.*

A Note from the Start-to-Finish® Editors

This book has been divided into approximately equal chapters so that the student can read a chapter and take a test or respond in writing after one reading session.

You will also notice that Start-to-Finish Books look different from other high-low readers and chapter books. The text layout of this book coordinates with the other media components (CD and audiocassette) of the Start-to-Finish series.

The text in the book matches, line for line and page for page, the text shown on the computer screen, enabling readers to follow along easily in the book. Each 2-page layout ends in a complete sentence so that the student can either practice the pages (repeat reading) or turn the page to continue with the story. Sometimes the last sentence at the bottom of the left hand page continues to the top of the right hand page. If the last sentence on the right hand page cannot fit on the page in its entirety, it has been shifted to the next page. For this reason, the sentence at the top of a page may not be indented, signaling that it is part of the paragraph from the preceding page.

Words are not hyphenated at the ends of lines. This sometimes creates extra space at the end of a line, but eliminates confusion for the struggling reader.